ALADDIN

Long ago, in a land far away, there lived a young boy called Aladdin and his widowed mother. They lived in a small village in China, and life was hard for them.

One day a strange man came to the village.

"Perhaps I will find what I'm looking for here," he muttered as he came to the houses and saw some boys playing.

"Aha!" he said. "I think my search is over." He watched for a few minutes, and then went up to the boys.

"Can you tell me where young Aladdin and his mother live?" he asked.

"I'm Aladdin," said Aladdin. "Why do you want to know?"

"My boy!" cried the man. "I'm your uncle, your father's brother! Take me to your mother."

Aladdin lived close by, so he led the way.

"Good morning," said the uncle to Aladdin's mother. "I'm your husband's brother, returned at last. Is my brother around?"

"He's dead," said Aladdin's mother. "It's been five years."

"I'm so sorry," said the man. "Can Aladdin help me this afternoon?"

"How?" asked Aladdin.

"There is a cave in the hillside above, and when we were small we hid something down there. I've come back to collect it and I'm too big to get in the hole. Maybe you can help. I'll give you a precious ring."

"Yes, I'll help you," said Aladdin. "How far is it?"

"Not far," said the uncle. "Let's go."

They climbed the hillside, and came to a small hole in the ground. The uncle was much too big to climb down, but Aladdin was just the right size.

"Here's the ring," said the uncle. Aladdin put it on.

"What am I looking for?" he asked.

"Oh, just an old lamp," said the uncle. "Battered looking. Not good for much, but I'd really like it back."

Aladdin climbed down the hole, and entered a cave that twinkled and shone from floor to ceiling with gold and jewels.

"There's treasure down here," called Aladdin.

"I know," said the uncle. "Just bring me the old lamp."

'How strange,' thought Aladdin. 'All this treasure and all he wants is an old lamp. Ah! There it is.'

Aladdin went back to the cave entrance.

"Do you have the lamp?" asked his uncle.

"Yes, give me a hand to get out," said Aladdin, holding up his hand.

"Give me the lamp, then I'll pull you out."

"Pull me out first," said Aladdin.

"I want the lamp," said the uncle, becoming angry.

"Why?" asked Aladdin. "It's tatty. All this treasure and you only want this?"

"Just give it to me," shouted the uncle.

"No, I won't," said Aladdin. "Help me out first!"

"Never!" said the uncle. "You can stay down there! Stay with the treasure!"

There was a sudden thunderclap, and the tunnel closed! Aladdin was trapped. He had the lamp and the treasure, but he couldn't get out.

"He's not my uncle," said Aladdin. He sat down and absentmindedly began to rub the ring his 'uncle' had given him.

There was a sudden flash of light and a puff of smoke, and a figure stood in front of him wearing a turban. How strange! And stranger still:

"Master of the ring! How can I serve you?" asked the figure.

"Who are you?" asked Aladdin.

"The Genie of the ring," said the figure. "How can I serve you?"

"Is it possible to take me home?" asked Aladdin.

"Your wish is my command."

A moment later, Aladdin was outside his cottage. He was still holding the lamp. He ran in

and told his mother of his adventure. Then he called up the Genie of the ring again. His mother nearly fell over in amazement.

"Can you bring some food, please?" said Aladdin.

A moment later, the table was groaning under the weight of lots of exotic dishes.

Aladdin and his mother ate and ate, and for the first time in a long while they went to bed well fed and happy.

Little by little, as the days passed, Aladdin made the cottage comfortable for his mother with the help of the Genie, and there was always plenty to eat.

One evening, by the fire, Aladdin's mother took the lamp. "We may as well use this," she said. "I'll give it a polish."

She began to rub with a cloth, when there was a huge thunderclap and a flash of light. In a puff of smoke a new figure appeared. He was much bigger than the Genie of the ring.

"Oh Master, how can I serve you?" asked the Genie.

Aladdin's mother was speechless.

"This is what the man was after," thought Aladdin, and then he quickly said, "Can you build us a new home just outside the village and please take us there."

"Your wish is my command," boomed the Genie.

An instant later, Aladdin and his mother were sitting in comfortable chairs beside a huge fire in their new home.

"I can't quite get used to the speed they do things," said Aladdin's mother.

The Genie of the lamp was much more powerful than the Genie of the ring, and soon there were servants and carriages, taking Aladdin and his mother wherever they wanted to go.

One day, Aladdin said to his mother, "It is time I married. I want to marry the Emperor's daughter."

"The Princess!" cried his mother. "You must be mad! You cannot marry the Princess!"

"I love her," said Aladdin. "I'd like you to take a present to the Emperor and ask him for his daughter's hand in marriage."

Aladdin finally persuaded his mother. She took with her a basket of fruit as a present. But these were no ordinary fruits. They were made of precious stones. It was a fabulous gift for the Emperor.

The Emperor was very impressed, but he did not want his daughter to marry a peasant's son.

Aladdin went to the palace the very next day, dressed finely, with a gift of six beautiful white horses.

"No," said the Emperor.

Aladdin went day after day, with the most amazing gifts. Each time the Emperor said, "No!"

The Princess had seen Aladdin and each day she fell more and more in love with him. She finally spoke to her father.

"Very well," he said. "I shall give him a task to perform. If he can do it you will both be married."

Aladdin arrived at the palace, and the Emperor gave him his task.

"I would like you to build the Princess a palace that she can live in," said the Emperor. "It must have four domes, two fine towers, marble staircases, a beautiful garden, and it must be joined to this palace by a crystal bridge."

"Very well," said Aladdin.

"That is not all," said the Emperor. "I want it built overnight. If you want to marry my daughter, the palace must be here by tomorrow morning."

Aladdin returned home and called up the Genie of the lamp. He described what the Emperor wanted.

"Your wish is my command," said the Genie.

The next morning, the Emperor awoke to find the tip of a crystal bridge against his balcony, and a beautiful palace shimmered in the distance. Everything he had asked for had been built. He was astounded, but the Princess made sure he kept his promise.

The Princess and Aladdin were married and lived happily in the palace.

Meanwhile, high in the mountains, the magician who had pretended to be Aladdin's uncle heard of the marvellous presents given to the Emperor by a peasant boy, and then of the fantastic palace.

"That is the work of the lamp," he said. He collected his belongings and prepared to go down into the valley in search of the lamp.

One day Aladdin went hunting and the Princess was in Aladdin's rooms and saw the lamp on a table.

"What a tatty looking lamp," she said. "How strange that Aladdin keeps it when he can so easily buy another."

A servant came to tell the Princess that there were travelling pedlars in the main hall.

"I might be able to buy a present for Aladdin," she said, running to the hall.

There were many traders there,

but one call caught her attention immediately.

"New lamps for old! New lamps for old!"

"That's what I shall do for Aladdin," said the Princess, and she ran to fetch the old lamp.

Aladdin returned from hunting later that day to find a very angry and worried Emperor, and no Princess, palace or lamp!

"You must bring back my daughter at once!" cried the Emperor.

Aladdin didn't know what to do! Without the Genie of the lamp, he was powerless.

Then he remembered the ring that he still wore. He rubbed it gently and the Genie appeared in his usual puff of smoke.

"Master of the ring! How can I serve you?" asked the Genie.

"Can you bring back the palace with the Princess?" asked Aladdin.

"Unfortunately, no," said the Genie. "That is the Genie of the lamp's magic."

"Can you take me there?" asked Aladdin.

"Yes," said the Genie, and in an

instant Aladdin was standing in a strange place with the Princess by his side.

"Aladdin!" she cried. "The magician told me you were dead."

"Well, I'm not," said Aladdin. "We must get the lamp back from him. It's the only way to get you back to your father."

"The magician never lets it out of his sight," said the Princess.

"We must wait until he is asleep and get it from him then," said Aladdin. He called the Genie of the ring and asked him for a sleeping potion.

The Princess put it in the magician's drink. He was soon yawning and fell fast asleep.

Aladdin took the lamp and called up the Genie.

"Take us and the palace back home," said Aladdin. "And as for the man who tricked us – leave him to wander the desert for ever."

"Your wish is my command," said the Genie.

A moment later the Princess and Aladdin were standing on the crystal bridge.

Everything was as it had been before and the Emperor was waiting with open arms to greet them.

The Emperor was delighted to see them. They were never troubled by the magician again, who is probably still wandering around the desert.

JACK AND THE BEANSTALK

Long ago, in a land far away, a poor woman and her only son Jack lived in a tumbledown house. One day the woman found that they had no food left at all and no money to buy any more.

"Jack!" called the woman.

"Yes, mother," said Jack, who was beginning to feel hungry.

"Jack, you must take the cow to market and sell her," said his mother. "Make sure that you get a good price for her, as she's all we have left and we need the money to buy food."

Jack went to the field and tied a rope around the cow's neck. The cow followed along behind Jack as he walked down the road towards the town.

Suddenly he was not alone. There was a small old man walking beside him. Jack was very surprised. Where had the man come from?

"That's a nice cow," said the strange man.

"Yes, she is," said Jack. "But she won't be ours for much longer."

"Why's that?" asked the old man.

"I'm off to market to sell her," said Jack.

"I'll buy her," said the old man.

"I must go to the market," said Jack. "I must get the best price I can."

"I'll give you a good price for her," said the man.

"How much?" asked Jack.

"Seven magic beans," said the man, and he held up a pouch.

"Beans!" exclaimed Jack.

"Magic beans," said the man. "I'll give you the beans for the cow, and life will be different for you."

"It certainly will be different," said Jack. "My mother would not be very happy if I came home with a handful of beans. I'm sorry, but I must sell her at the market."

"You will not be very successful," said the man. "But go if you must. I'll see you later. Goodbye."

"Goodbye," said Jack, and he carried on into town.

The market was very busy, and Jack stood in the middle, calling out that his cow was for sale. But nobody spoke to him, or even looked at the cow.

"I'm asking a good price," he called.

But no-one bought the cow. At the end of the afternoon everyone started packing up.

Jack still had his cow.

"Come on," he said to the cow. "I'll have to take you home."

As he walked, the strange little man appeared again.

"You still have your cow," he said to Jack. "I still have the seven magic beans."

Jack stopped and thought. 'If I go home with the cow, we'll have nothing to eat. But if the beans really are magic, then maybe things will change.'

"Very well," he said. "I'll take the beans."

"A wise choice," said the old man. "Good luck, and goodbye."

"Thank you for the beans," said Jack, and he headed for home. He looked back once, but the strange man was nowhere to be seen.

"Beans!" shouted his mother, when she saw what Jack had been given for the cow. "How will beans feed us?"

"They're magic beans," said Jack.

"Magic! How stupid!" said his mother.

"Oh, you silly boy!" And she threw the beans out of the window.

They both went to bed hungry.

When Jack woke the next morning, the light through his window was green.

"How strange," said Jack, and he went to the window. A strange sight met his eyes. A huge green trunk was growing past his window, with enormous leaves, blocking out the light.

"Jack!" called his mother. "What is it?"

Jack ran downstairs and looked outside.

"It's the beans!" he said. "There's an enormous beanstalk growing just where you threw the beans last night. Look how high it is."

They both looked up and the beanstalk seemed to be growing right up into the sky, disappearing into the clouds.

"I'm going to climb it," said Jack suddenly.

"Oh, Jack," said his mother. "Is that a good idea? You don't know where it goes."

"I'll find out," said Jack. He went to the base of the beanstalk and began climbing.

"That man said life would be different," Jack called, and he climbed up and up.

Jack climbed so high that he went through the damp,

white clouds. On the other side, the beanstalk finished. A path stretched away in front of Jack. In the distance he could see a castle.

When he reached the castle, he stood before the enormous gate and pulled on the bell.

A large woman came to the door.

"How did you get here?" she asked. "Come in quickly, before my husband arrives home."

Jack was taken into the kitchen.

Everything seemed to be enormous. The table and chair were like mountains to him.

"You must be hungry," said the woman. "Have some breakfast."

Jack was given a plate of food and he tucked into it as the climb had made him very hungry.

Loud footsteps could suddenly be heard.

"That's my husband," said the woman. "You must hide. He will eat a small boy like you."

Jack hid behind the oven door,
but watched to see who came in.

"FEE, FI, FO, FUM,
    I smell the blood of an Englishman.
Be he alive or be he dead,
    I'll grind his bones to make my bread!"

shouted the giant as he came into the kitchen.

"You're imagining things," said his wife. "There's no Englishman here. Your breakfast is on the table."

Jack watched as the giant sat and ate his breakfast. Every so often he stopped and sniffed. He muttered and then carried on eating.

Finally, when he was full, he called out to his wife, "Bring me my golden hen!"

The hen was tiny, and sat on the table in front of the giant.

"Lay, golden hen!" said the giant. The hen began to lay eggs, but they were golden eggs.

Jack looked at this from his hiding place.

'My mother would like a hen like that,' he thought, and he watched and waited.

The giant was full from his breakfast, and soon he began to snore. Before long he was fast asleep.

This was Jack's chance. He jumped up and climbed on to the table. He crept past the giant, picked up the hen and then ran. He ran as fast as he could, out of the castle, along the path, and then down the beanstalk.

His mother was very relieved to see him, and she was delighted with the hen that laid golden eggs. They would never go hungry again.

Jack began to get bored after a while. All their money problems were solved and they now had plenty to eat and new clothes to wear.

One day, he said to his mother, "I'm going to climb the beanstalk again."

"But why?" she asked. "We have all we need."

"I want to see what else is up there," said Jack, and he climbed the beanstalk once again.

This time when he reached the castle, he crept in and hid in a drawer.

After a while, he heard the loud footsteps.

"FEE, FI, FO, FUM,

    I smell the blood of an Englishman.

Be he alive or be he dead,

    I'll grind his bones to make my bread!"

boomed the giant. "This time I'll find him."

"I'll help you," said his wife. "The naughty boy took your favourite hen."

The giant and his wife looked high and low, but they did not find Jack.

"Don't upset yourself any more, my dear," said the giant's wife. "Eat your dinner, and then have a rest."

The giant sat down and began to eat.

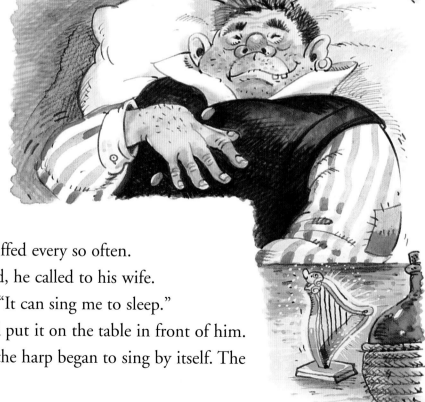

Jack was in the drawer right underneath his nose. The giant sniffed every so often.

When he had finished his food, he called to his wife.

"Bring me my harp," he said. "It can sing me to sleep."

His wife brought the harp and put it on the table in front of him. The giant stroked the strings and the harp began to sing by itself. The giant smiled, and yawned.

The harp sang and sang, and soon the giant was snoring.

Jack thought the harp was the most beautiful thing he had ever seen.

As soon as the giant was fast asleep, he jumped out of the drawer and grabbed the harp.

"Master! Master!" shouted the harp, "Help me!"

Jack had to run faster than ever before.

The giant leapt up from his chair, shouting "FEE, FI, FO, FUM!" He ran after Jack, out through the door and along the path.

Jack ran as fast as he could, and when he came to the beanstalk, he started down it without stopping for breath. The beanstalk began to shake as the roaring giant climbed down after him.

"Mother!" called Jack, as soon as he could see the cottage beneath him. "Mother, bring me an axe!"

His mother took one look up the beanstalk and ran to fetch an axe.

When Jack was on the ground, his mother took the harp and handed him the axe.

WHACK! WHACK! went the axe, cutting into the beanstalk.

"Faster!" cried his mother

"FEE, FI, FO, FUM!" bellowed the giant. WHACK! the axe cut through the beanstalk and suddenly the whole thing began to fall over.

Over it went, taking the giant with it!

CRASH! The beanstalk landed on the ground, making a huge hole and the giant tumbled down the hole, never to be seen again.

Jack and his mother lived happily ever after. With the golden hen they never had to worry about money again and Jack had the harp to sing him off to sleep every night.

PINOCCHIO

O ne day a carpenter picked up a log of wood from a pile in the corner of his workshop. He was just about to chop it with his axe when he heard a little voice cry, "Don't hurt me!" The voice came from the log of wood.

The carpenter was so terrified that he opened the door and was about to throw the log away, when who should come by, but Geppetto the toy maker.

"Just what I need," cried the old man. "I am going to carve a puppet that will behave just like a real boy."

The carpenter was pleased to get rid of

the talking log, because he thought it was bewitched!

Back at his toy shop Geppetto started work straight away. First he carved the puppet's head with great care and as he was putting the finishing touches to the face a most amazing thing happened . . . the eyes blinked and the mouth smiled!

Geppetto eagerly started work on the puppet's body and carefully worked his way down to the toes.

All of a sudden the puppet's foot flew up and kicked the old man on the nose! Instead of being angry, Geppetto was delighted with his moving puppet.

"I shall call you Pinocchio," he smiled, "and you shall call me Father."

Without delay,

Geppetto began to teach Pinocchio how to walk. No sooner had the cheeky puppet learned, than he dashed out of the door and ran off down the street. Suddenly, a large policeman

stepped out in front of Pinocchio and grabbed him.

By now quite a crowd had gathered and Geppetto was shouting at Pinocchio for running away. The angry crowd told the policeman to lock the old man up, for they thought that he was being cruel to the little puppet.

So the policeman took poor Geppetto away to prison and Pinocchio ran off home.

You will have guessed by now that Pinocchio had a mind of his own and was going to do exactly as he pleased!

Later on, poor old Geppetto was let out of prison because the policeman realised that he had done nothing wrong. He made Pinocchio promise that he would go to school and learn to read.

That night, Geppetto made him some new clothes.

"All I need now, Father, is a spelling book," said Pinocchio. "Then I shall

be like other boys."

At once, the kind old man went out into the cold night and sold his only coat to buy the spelling book for the puppet boy.

Next morning, Pinocchio set off on his way to school with the new book in his wooden hand. But what was that wonderful sound that he could hear? It was the music of a

34

fairground! Pinocchio excitedly went to investigate and when he spotted a Puppet Theatre you might guess that he instantly forgot all about school. Without so much as a second thought Pinocchio sold his spelling book to buy a ticket to go inside.

But when the other puppets saw Pinocchio, they shouted for him to come up on stage to join them. Of course, the whole performance was quite ruined! The puppeteer was very angry with Pinocchio and threatened to throw him on the fire, like a log of wood.

However, Pinocchio cried so miserably at this that the puppeteer at last took pity on

him and gave him five pieces of gold to take home to Geppetto.

On his way back home, Pinocchio met a sly fox and a cat who pretended to be blind. They told the puppet that if he buried his gold in a certain field, a miracle would happen – a magic tree would grow, laden with gold pieces and make him rich beyond his wildest dreams!

It was a trick, of course! But silly little Pinocchio believed them and buried the coins just as they had said. Naturally, when Pinocchio returned the next day, the five gold pieces had gone

and so had the fox and the cat.

Not content with stealing Pinocchio's money, the fox and the cat disguised themselves as robbers and grabbed Pinocchio. They hung him from a tree and then ran off and left him there.

Luckily for Pinocchio, the Blue Fairy lived nearby and she saved him. As Pinocchio did not seem quite well she sent her little poodle dog to fetch the doctors to see what was the

matter with him . . . and what strange doctors they turned out to be . . . a crow, an owl and a cricket!

They all decided that Pinocchio was not dead after all, he was just a wicked wooden puppet that had run away.

The Blue Fairy then asked Pinocchio to tell her about his adventures, but the silly little puppet would not tell the truth. The more he lied, the

longer his nose grew. Indeed it grew so long that it stuck right out of the window!

At this, the Blue Fairy clapped her hands and several birds flew down. They pecked at Pinocchio's nose until it was the right size once more.

"That's what comes of telling lies!" laughed the Blue Fairy.

"How can I become a real boy?" Pinocchio asked the Blue Fairy.

"If you are good and go to school, you will have your dearest wish,"

she promised.

So Pinocchio went back to school. He worked hard, but unfortunately he soon grew tired of being good. He made friends with the naughtiest boy in the class.

One night they decided to run away to Toyland (where there is no school). They climbed into a special coach pulled by donkeys, and off they went in high spirits.

It seemed fun at first, having no lessons and no work at all – nothing to do all day but mess around and play. Lazy Pinocchio and his naughty young friend just loved it!

Then, without warning, Pinocchio woke up one day to find he had grown a pair of donkey's ears. His friend had already changed into a donkey. All the children who came to Toyland were changed into donkeys and then sold.

A circus ringmaster bought poor Pinocchio and worked him very hard. One day, when he was jumping through a hoop, he hurt his leg.

The circus didn't want a lame donkey, so Pinocchio was sold again, this time to a man who wanted to make the donkey's skin into a drum.

He dragged Pinocchio into the sea to drown him, but the cheeky puppet slipped out of the skin and swam away laughing.

But as he was swimming in the water, suddenly a gigantic whale rose up from the waves. Its

monstrous jaws opened up wide and swallowed up Pinocchio in one gulp.

Down and down went the puppet right to the bottom of the whale's stomach. He felt very

frightened, until he heard a voice he knew.

There was old Geppetto, the carpenter, sitting in a small wooden boat, carving toys from the fish bones lying all around.

Geppetto jumped up and hugged the little puppet to him in joy. He explained that he had gone to sea to look for Pinocchio and, just like the puppet, had been swallowed up whole by the enormous whale. Since then he had been living on the food that he had packed in his boat.

With the help of the Blue Fairy, the two sailed out of the whale's mouth and not long afterwards they arrived safely back home again.

Pinocchio sat down with Geppetto and told him all about his adventures in Toyland, and he promised faithfully never to leave the kind old man again.

During the night, when Pinocchio was asleep, the Blue Fairy came by and granted Pinocchio his wish. When he woke the next morning, he had become a real boy at last!